Number Seven

Dorling Kinderlsey
www.dk.com

Editor Fiona Munro
Designer Lisa Hollis

Published in Great Britain in 1997
by Dorling Kindersley Limited, 9 Henrietta St, London WC2E 8PS
This edition published in 2000

A CIP catalogue record for this book is available from the British Library.

ISBN 0-7513-6707-9

Color reproduction by DOT Gradations
Printed in Hong Kong by Wing King Tong

Number Seven

COLIN AND JACQUI HAWKINS

Dorling Kindersley

"I'm the brightest spark in Numbertown!" said Number Seven.

Hello !

She lived in a large house with an orange roof. It had seven windows and seven blue chimney-pots. It was the seventh house in Numbertown. The address was 7, Number Lane.

Number Seven was a very clever inventor.

She had invented a
toaster to toast seven
pieces of bread,
a straw to drink seven
drinks at once,

a seven hour timer, and a vacuum cleaner that could do seven different sorts of cleaning.

Every morning at seven o'clock, Number
Seven was woken by Robbie the Robot.
Robbie was Number Seven's most
useful invention. He had seven eyes,
seven arms and seven legs.

I am
Robbie.

"Wake up, Number Seven. Time to get up.
There's work to do for me and you!"
bleeped Robbie.

"What shall I invent today?" said Number Seven. She went to work with seven brilliant ideas buzzing in her head.

What a good idea!

Seven minutes later, she was hard at work in her laboratory. The machines whirred and purred.

Hum! Hiss! Ping! Zing!

Number Seven lifted levers, wiggled wires and spun spanners. "I'm a bright spark," she said.

In Number Seven's laboratory, there was
a big heavy door. Behind the door was
her new invention. It was bright red,
and it could fly to the moon!

Shh !

"Hussssssh!"

whispered Number Seven.
"It's top secret, but goes like a rocket!"

"All aboard," said Number Seven, as she sat
at the controls of the red spaceship.

"7, 6, 5, 4, 3, 2, 1 . . . BLAST OFF !"

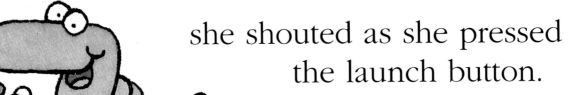

she shouted as she pressed
the launch button.

Whoosh!

The spaceship roared out
through the roof and whizzed high into
the sky above Numbertown.

"This is heaven!"
said Number Seven.

Higher and higher went the red spaceship, leaving the earth far below. "Dizzy, whizzy me! It's out of this world," whooped Number Seven as she whizzed around the moon seven times.

Whizz! Whizz! Whizz! Whizz! Whizz! Whizz! Whizz!

"I'm in heaven!" said Number Seven.

"Goodbye moon. I'll see you soon," sang Number Seven as the spaceship zoomed off.
"Are you going to go far?" asked the moon.
"Just to the stars," said Number Seven, and seven minutes later she was twirling and whirling around seven shining stars. "You're a star turn," they twinkled.

Bye!

Bye!

"I'm in heaven!" said Number Seven.

All too soon it was time to leave the stars and head for home.
"Ta-ra, stars," said Number Seven.
The stars waved goodbye.

"Time to go home!"

"Get ready rocket:

7, 6, 5, 4, 3, 2, 1 . . . GO!"

boomed Number Seven.

Whoosh!

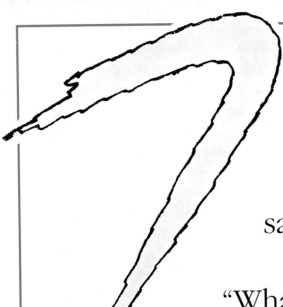

The red rocket zoomed
homewards and landed
safely back in Numbertown.
"Have you been far?"
"What was it like?" asked the
Numberlies as they gathered round.

"It was heaven!"
said Number Seven.

All the Numberlies clapped and cheered.

"Hurrah for Number Seven,
the first Numberlie in space!"